Old Pearl

Wendy Wahman

Old Pearl

atheneum

A CAITLYN DLOUHY BOOK

Atheneum Books for Young Readers • New York London Toronto Sydney New Delhi

Theo loved feeding the birds.
All the birds. But he tried his hardest
to aim his seeds toward the bird
with the raggedy wing.

But no matter how close Theo got,
a quicker bird pecked up
the seeds first.

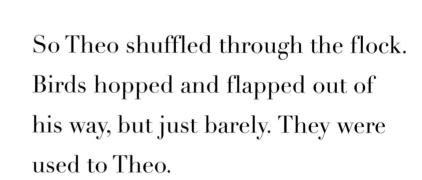

So Theo shuffled through the flock.
Birds hopped and flapped out of
his way, but just barely. They were
used to Theo.

Waving the other birds aside, Theo knelt down.

"You're a tough old bird. That's what my Grandma Pearl
would say, anyway. A tough old bird, just like her."

"Here you go, Pearl.
These are all for you."

Suddenly, a voice shouted,

"No, Jasper, nooo!
Bad dog, come!"
The birds scattered.

All except one.

"Fly!" Theo called out, shooing with his arms. But the bird just blinked at him and swayed side to side.

"Go! *Fly!* Can't you fly?!"

Theo scooped her up just as the dog leapt.

"Oh, hey, sorry about that," said Jasper's owner.

"Is your bird okay?"

"She's not my . . ." *She's not my bird.*
That's what Theo was going to say.
But holding her little self in his
arms—he knew that wasn't true.

"Theo, you can't bring that bird inside,"
said Grandma Pearl when he came home.

"Grandma, she can't fly. A dog nearly caught her!"
said Theo.

Grandma leaned close. "Is she hurt?"

"Nah, I saved her. And I named her Pearl."

"Oh, you didn't!" Grandma chuckled. "Alright. Why don't we watch her for the night, to make sure she's okay. But tomorrow she goes straight back where you found her."

Grandma set up Theo's old playpen, and Theo brought Pearl dinner.

Later, Grandma tucked Theo into bed. "Good night, Theo. Sweet dreams."

"Good night, Pearl," said Theo.
"Sweet dreams."

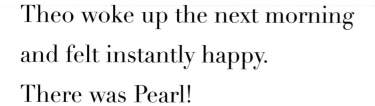

Theo woke up the next morning
and felt instantly happy.
There was Pearl!

Then he felt instantly less happy.
Today he had to take Pearl back
to the park.

But at breakfast, Grandma said, "I've been thinking. Before we let Pearl back in the wild, we should have that wing checked. I wish there were a bird rescue nearby, or even an animal shelter. Hmmm. Oh, I know where we can take her!"

The veterinarian examined Pearl, beak to toe.
Theo made sure the vet was extra gentle.

"Nothing out of the ordinary," said the doctor, "except this
bum wing that's got her grounded. She's just old.
And you know what they say: *Old age is not an illness.*"

She and Grandma laughed.

In the car, Grandma said, "Time to bring Pearl
back to the park."

"Why?! She needs us. She can't fly."

"Theo, she's a wild bird. She's been free all her life."

"Her life . . . that I saved."

"That's how it is in nature, Theo," Grandma said gently.

"But, if we can do something about it . . . shouldn't we, Grandma?"

Grandma didn't say anything for a long, long time.

But she also drove straight past
the park without stopping.

She stopped somewhere else instead.

Back home, Theo made a clean, safe space for Pearl.

He kept her water fresh and her food dish full,

and he gave her toys to play with.

Pearl seemed *very* happy.

Sometimes they
went to the park.

Other times, Pearl seemed too tired to go far.

But Theo didn't mind, as long as he was with Pearl.

What Pearl liked best?

Sitting on Theo. Heartbeat to heartbeat.

Every morning, Theo and Pearl
shared apples with peanut butter.

And every night, Theo'd say,
"Good night, Pearl, sweet dreams."

One morning, though,
Pearl did not wake from
her sweet dreams.

When Grandma asked Theo
if he'd like to go to the park,
his answer was always the same:
"Maybe tomorrow."

As tomorrows came and went,
Theo's memories of Pearl turned
from tears to smiles.

At last, together, Theo and Grandma said goodbye to Pearl.

It was Theo's first day back
to the park. The birds—
the regulars and some
new friends—were there,
happy to see him.

Theo aimed his seeds for the one-legged bird at the back.

In loving memory of my mother,
Phyllis

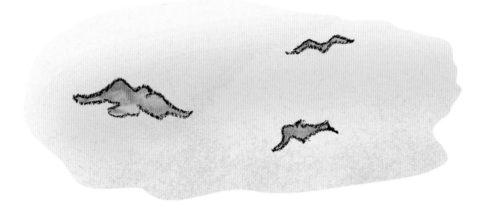

In this fictional story, Theo felt he had to protect Pearl when Jasper ran in. But in real life, it might not be as simple. An injured animal, even a friend like Pearl, might defend itself and could hurt you. And sometimes picking up an animal that seems to need help can cause it more harm. So if you come upon an injured animal, try your best to find an adult to help you do the right thing. You can learn all about what to do on these websites:

The Audubon Society: audubon.org or The Humane Society: humanesociety.org

ATHENEUM BOOKS FOR YOUNG READERS • An imprint of Simon & Schuster Children's Publishing Division • 1230 Avenue of the Americas, New York, New York 10020 • © 2021 by Wendy Wahman • Book design by Lauren Rille © 2021 by Simon & Schuster, Inc. • All rights reserved, including the right of reproduction in whole or in part in any form. • ATHENEUM BOOKS FOR YOUNG READERS is a registered trademark of Simon & Schuster, Inc. Atheneum logo is a trademark of Simon & Schuster, Inc. • For information about special discounts for bulk purchases, please contact Simon & Schuster Special Sales at 1-866-506-1949 or business@simonandschuster.com. • The Simon & Schuster Speakers Bureau can bring authors to your live event. For more information or to book an event, contact the Simon & Schuster Speakers Bureau at 1-866-248-3049 or visit our website at www.simonspeakers.com. • The text for this book was set in Didot. • The illustrations for this book were rendered in charcoal pencil and watercolor, and digitally collaged. • Manufactured in China • 0321 SCP • First Edition • 10 9 8 7 6 5 4 3 2 1 • Library of Congress Cataloging-in-Publication Data • Names: Wahman, Wendy, author. • Title: Old Pearl / Wendy Wahman. • Description: First edition. | New York : Atheneum Books for Young Readers, [2021] | Audience: Ages 4–8. | Audience: Grades K–1. | Summary: After Theo rescues an old, injured bird he names Pearl, he persuades his grandmother they should take care of her, and their special bond grows until Pearl passes away. • Identifiers: LCCN 2020016537 (print) | LCCN 2020016538 (eBook) | ISBN 9781534462694 (hardcover) | ISBN 9781534462700 (eBook) • Subjects: CYAC: Human-animal relationships—Fiction. | Birds—Fiction. | Old age—Fiction. | Wildlife rescue—Fiction. • Classification: LCC PZ7.W1269 Old 2021 (print) | LCC PZ7.W1269 (eBook) | DDC [E]—dc23 • LC record available at https://lccn.loc.gov/2020016537 • LC ebook record available at https://lccn.loc.gov/2020016538